EAT YOUR HEART OUT

A DARK ROMCOM

SYBIL KNIGHT

SOCIALS:

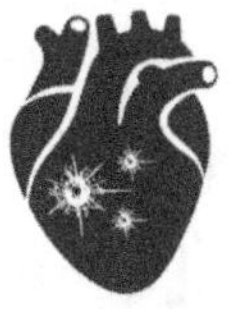

Email: authorsybilknight@gmail.com

Newsletter: www.sendfox.com/dahliaandsybil

Facebook Group:
www.facebook.com/groups/dahliaandsybilslittedevils

Instagram: www.instragram.com/author.sybil.knight

Facebook Page: www.facebook.com/authorsybilknight

TikTok: www.tiktok.com/@queensofchaosbooks

Amazon: https://www.amazon.com/stores/Sybil-Knight/author/B09QW5R3MB

NOTE FROM THE AUTHOR:

Look, this is gonna be dark, smutty, and completely ridiculous. So don't think about it too much and just enjoy the ride.

Now imagine if Dexter were a female cannibal...

DEDICATION

To the FBI guy assigned to monitor my search history who likely became concerned for my mental health when he saw me Google the word "cannibal" one too many times. My bad.

TRIGGER WARNING:

PLEASE BE ADVISED THAT THE FEMALE LEAD IN THIS BOOK IS… WELL, SHE'S "SLIGHTLY" UNHINGED TO PUT IT MILDLY. BUT AT LEAST SHE DOESN'T BREAK INTO PEOPLE'S HOUSES—*THAT'S THE MALE LEAD FOR YOU.*

WITH THIS IN MIND, THE AUTHOR ASKS THAT YOU HEED THE FOLLOWING LIST OF POTENTIAL TRIGGERS:

- OVERALL SEXUALLY EXPLICIT & VIOLENT CONTENT
- CANNIBALISM (INTENTIONAL & UNINTENTIONAL)
- DEATH & MURDER
- DESECRATION/ IMPROPER DISPOSAL OF A CORPSE(S)
- GRAPHIC INJURIES
- STALKING/ B&E
- TATTLING TO MOTHER
- OVERUSE OF SOUTHERN EUPHEMISMS (TRUST ME)
- LIGHT BLOOD PLAY
- NONCONSENSUAL USE OF A MAKESHIFT COCK RING

- MENTAL HEALTH REP
- DUBCON/CNC
- EDGING
- USE OF POISON
- MENTIONS OF GAMBLING ADDICTION
- MENTIONS OF ALCOHOL AND DRUG USE/ ABUSE
- BONDAGE
- MASKED ASSAILANT
- OBSESSION WITH DOLLY PARTON
- "TITANIC" REFERENCES
- OVERUSE OF HAIR SPRAY
- AND MORE...

THE HIGHER THE HAIR, THE CLOSER TO GOD.

—DOLLY PARTON

BLURB:

I didn't eat people. Just men.

First of all, I'd like to set the record straight. I wasn't a cannibal, 'kay?

I didn't eat *people*. Just men. I ate their hearts out before they ever saw me coming. Figuratively, of course. Most of the time.

Sometimes a girl had to do what a girl had to do. And sometimes what I had to do was fry those suckers up with a little bit of buttermilk and enough shortening to give ya coronary.

I wouldn't ever apologize for it.

Which was something else you should know about me. I was unapologetic. Then again, so was he. Else the

HOTSHOT WITH A BLADE BIGGER THAN HIS DICK WOULDN'T HAVE BARGED HIS WAY INTO MY LITTLE APARTMENT WITHOUT SO MUCH AS A "MY BAD, SORRY FOR DISTURBING YOU, MA'AM."

AND I WOULDN'T HAVE BEEN FORCED TO TIE HIM TO A CHAIR AND TEACH HIM SOME MANNERS. BUT HERE WE ARE, AIN'T WE?

JUST A SWEET LITTLE SOUTHERN GIRL AND THE BIG BAD PICKLE-DIDDLER WHO THOUGHT HE WAS ABOUT TO GET HIS ROCKS OFF.

GUESS IT WASN'T HIS LUCKY DAY. SURE WAS MINE, THOUGH.

EAT YOUR HEART OUT IS A DARK STANDALONE NOVELLA WITH A HEA. PLEASE HEED THE TRIGGER WARNINGS AT THE BEGINNING OF THE BOOK.

CHAPTER ONE
CHARLEE

Sugar and spice and everything nice, that was what little girls were made of...

I glanced down at the severed hand I was tryin' my darnedest to force down the garbage disposal and cocked a hip.

Guess my mama got the recipe wrong. Too much spice and not enough nice. Then again, Jimmy here wasn't being very nice when he tried to grip me up in the Wally's parking lot last night, now was he?

I grabbed on to the flat side of the wooden spatula and did my best to force the rest of his fingers into the drain. But those darn knuckle joints just kept getting caught up on the blades.

I sighed and gave it another go. Using the full weight of my upper body, girls included, to press on the handle and dislodge the pesky piece of cartilage that seemed to be jamming everything up. As soon as I heard the motor rev back to life, I pulled the spatula away to keep her from going down with it.

"Voilà!"

The grinding sound was music to my ears after all the fuss The Mad Grabber was giving me since I had no choice but to *give him* a lesson in manners.

Mighta seemed a little cruel. To leave a man bleeding out in the alleyway behind a hospital, but it was the only way to teach him the most important rule 'round here: If you don't know how to play with your toys, you don't get to keep 'em.

And that included your hands or any other body part that didn't know how to behave itself.

Hearts were a little harder. Couldn't do much with the rest of the body once you took a guy's heart. Well, the docs couldn't. I could do plenty. Which was why my freezer was chock-full of man meat. Rib cages, thigh chunks, flanks and loins...

My stomach growled at the thought, so I turned off the garbage disposal, tossed the spatula into the sink, and popped open the fridge. My eyes bouncing over each of the handwritten labels I'd stuck on the sides of the white butcher paper before they landed on the one in the far left corner.

Philip. Now, that guy was a real sweetheart. 'Cause of the diabetes. Not his demeanor. In that case, he'd been one of the biggest assholes I'd ever met. Which was why I'd turned his rear end into lunchmeat. His torso too. While the rest of him was used as fertilizer for my rose garden.

There was nothing prettier than the roses I could see outside my kitchen window, 'cept maybe the nice sear I got when I dropped a piece of fresh thigh meat onto a hot griddle.

I swiped up a packet of Philip and deposited it on the counter before scouring the cupboards for my favorite pan. I was just about to drop old rusty onto the stove when I heard the rattling of my front door knob, glanced at the monitor for the motion-activated camera I'd set up a few weeks back, and decided I had a much better use for the cast-iron skillet I was currently clutching in my hand.

CHAPTER TWO
JACK

ucking hell...

My head was pounding and not the kind of pounding that came with a long night of trying to drink my problems away. Or the kind of pounding that told me I'd let some broad use me up and spit me out like the kids I shot down her throat. Nope, this was the kind that came with an ID bracelet, a shit-ton of drugs, and a hospital bill twice the size of Marla's fake tits.

For reference, Marla wasn't some broad. She was my cousin Tony's girl, and it wasn't that I looked at her like that or nothing. She was fucking family, and family was ona the few lines I didn't cross. It was just that when she was in the room, there was nowhere else to look. It was like something outta that *Black Mirror* show.

You turned to the left. Tits. To the right. More tits. Turned all the way the fuck around, and guess what? Fucking tits. Those UFOs of hers practically sucked the eyeballs out ya sockets. Which pissed Tony the fuck off.

Not sure why, seeing as he was the one who'd fronted the bill in the first place.

Didn't matter. Point was, my head was jacked all the way up, and no insurance meant I was probably spread out behind some bar somewhere.

My first instinct was to check for my wallet. Except that was hard to do with my arms tied behind my back and my feet strapped to the legs of a chair. I tried to rock back and forth a few times, tip myself over without bothering to open an eye. Mostly because both were glued shut by the dried blood I now realized was caked all over my black ski mask.

"I wouldn't do that if I were you."

I stopped what I was doing, not because she told me to do it. But because she was a... *she* and I didn't remember if I agreed to some weird bondage shit or if I'd finally pissed off the wrong chick and this was my punishment for not calling her back. Both options were just as likely.

"Yeah? And why's that?" I asked the disembodied voice.

I could hear whoever it was shuffling around what sounded like a kitchen. Banging pots and pans, taking shit out of cabinets and slamming 'em down on the counter before she came stomping towards me. Legit stomping. It was how I knew she was coming. The clanking of high-heeled shoes against what I assumed was a tile floor.

By the time she was close enough that I could smell her perfume—a mix of something sweet and spicy, though I couldn't tell ya what was what—Miss Attitude was already gripping me up. Prying my swollen eyelid open through my mask and staring at me from the other side of the blood-tinted haze.

Blonde hair, all teased out and curled up like one of those beauty pageant girls. Blue eyes, thick lashes, and tits—well, let's just say if Marla's had their own orbit, this chick's could block out the sun.

She dropped my eyelid and I heard the way her hair brushed over her shoulders when she spun back around. " 'Cause all that bruisin's bad for the meat, honey."

CHAPTER THREE
CHARLEE

"Meat?"

I hadn't stuttered and obviously my little impromptu dinner guest had heard me well enough to be repeating me. But I couldn't blame 'em for asking. Blows to the head had this way of making things foggy.

Instead of answering him, I strolled over to the fridge and tugged the door open. "Really don't have much room left in the freezer but Mama always said: *Waste not want not, Charlee.*"

"Charlee? Ain't that a guy's name?" he muttered to himself.

I leaned forward, being sure to give my new friend a direct view up my short-shorts as I shuffled a few packages from one shelf to the other, mindful of the dates on the top. Nothing was worse than getting a mouthful of spoiled meat, 'cept if maybe that meat had your name on it.

I paused to glance over a shoulder, noticing the way his eyes were honed in on my backside. "That's awfully sexist coming from someone who got beat up by a girl."

"Catching a guy unawares ain't exactly fair play, *Charlee*." He grinned through the swelling in his jaw. I could see the movement beneath the ski mask he was wearing like some third-rate Hamburglar.

I slammed the fridge shut and spun around, clicking my pink boot heels against the kitchen floor as I closed the distance. "Breaking into a gal's house ain't exactly fair play either..." I placed one hand on the armrest, the other reaching around and digging into his pockets. Once I tugged his wallet free, I thumbed through that until I found his ID and dropped it on the kitchen table. "Jack Dawson? Really?" I snorted.

He shrugged a single shoulder. "What can I say? My ma was a big Leo fan back in the day."

"Then why didn't she name you Leo?" I yanked the mask off his head and watched a slow trickle of blood trail down his brow, my eyes bouncing from the ID back to the face in front of me.

Same guy. Wasn't all that bad looking either. As far as home invaders went.

"How the hell am I supposed to know? Why don'tcha ask her?" he grunted while trying to blow some of the blood away from his pursed mouth.

Keep doing that and you'll give yourself age lines, sugar.

I tsked my tongue but kept my thoughts to myself as I leaned forward again and flicked my tongue out to clean it up for him, at the same time my hand was plucking his phone from the front of his leather jacket. I'd searched all his pockets before I'd tied him up. It was always much more fun for them to watch me do it, though. Their faces lighting up brighter than a tot at a magic show.

"Okay, I will." I grinned, flipping my hair over a shoulder as I pivoted on a heel and made my way towards the bedroom. Ya know, in case the mama's boy thought screaming out for help was a good idea.

"Wait, what? What are you doing?" he shouted after me. "Don't you dare call my mother!"

CHAPTER FOUR
JACK

S*he wouldn't, would she? I mean, what kind of lunatic ties you up, clips your phone, and then uses it to call your mother?*

"She said you don't call her enough. Oh, and she woulda named you Leo but unfortunately your pa's last name wasn't DiCaprio." Barbie came strutting back into the kitchen with her hands on her hips before tossing my cell on the table beside us.

Who would do that? Oh, right, the lunatic standing in front of me would.

Normally, I'd assume the broad was lying out her ass. But that sounded exactly like something my ma would say.

I glanced from my phone to Charlee's expectant glare. My mouth curling into a grin as I tapped into that Dawson charm my old man and I were both known for. "You've seen my face—you've had a nice little chat with my mother—don't ya think it's time you let me go now, sweetheart?"

She quirked a brow at me, her arms moving from her hips to fold over her chest. I craned my neck to the side and watched the way her cleavage popped out of her crop top. Things weren't looking great for me, but they could be worse, I guess.

"Look, babe, it was nothing personal..." I tried again, and immediately realized my mistake when she swung out a hand to slap me up the side of the head.

"Breaking into a gal's home sounds awfully personal to me," she countered.

"We're back on that, huh?" I grunted, spitting out another mouthful of blood and maybe a piece of tooth.

She turned around and continued stirring something she had out on the stovetop, lifting the spoon to her lips before adding another pinch of seasoning to the mixture. Smelled a little rancid if ya asked me, but I knew better than to critique a woman's cooking.

My old man taught me that too. He'd critiqued my mother's cooking once and only once. Still had a scar from where the side of the plate caught him under the eye before he could dodge it.

"You were gonna come in here and do nefarious things," Charlee hummed without bothering to look in my direction.

Nefarious things? It took a moment for my brain to catch up. "What? No!"

I was a bad guy, sure, but I wasn't that kind of *bad*

guy. I didn't need to go prowling for pussy with looks like these.

Charlee glanced at me over a shoulder again, her bright-blue eyes shadowed by a stray lock of hair. "So you were breaking in to do nice things?"

She gestured to the hunting knife I brought along in case a neighbor got curious (or brave or just plain stupid) and I had to scare 'em. Never had to use the damn thing for more than a little show and tell. Pretty-pretty princess here didn't need to know that, though.

"Well, I mean..." I grumbled.

"Fix the leaky pipe in the basement, hang a few shelves... Just a regular ol' Robin Hood with a rachet, aren't ya?" she huffed, and I cocked a swollen eyebrow.

"How exactly am I supposed to hang shelves with a ratchet?"

"Not the point," she barked, and I couldn't stop myself from chuckling.

"I was here to rob you, sweetheart. Not fuck you."

Maybe it was a heavy dose of brain damage. Maybe it was the fact this broad was cute when she was mad. Either way, by the time she crossed the room again, I was full-blown belly laughing in her face. And she seemed to like that even less than she like the idea of me pillaging her purse straps instead of her pussy lips.

CHAPTER FIVE
JACK

I expected another slap to the face. Would have deserved it too. Ma always did tell me my mouth would get me in trouble ona these days. What I didn't expect was to watch as Charlee dropped to her knees, unbuttoned my pants, reached a hand inside my boxers, and freed my cock.

Didn't matter how much blood was still coming out of the gash in my temple when most of it was redirected to my lap right now.

She opened her mouth, her tongue flicking forward without touching, and I lifted my ass off the chair to meet her halfway. That was all it took for this girl to unhinge her jaw like my cousin Mikey's ball python and swallow me whole like the pinkie mouse he dangled in front of it once a week.

Poof. Now ya see it, now ya don't. Leaving me to watch the up and down motion of her head bobbing against my crotch.

Usually I would be fisting her hair, guiding her rhythm until I found something I liked. But not too much. I wanted that shit to last. I wanted to enjoy it. Prolong the orgasm so that by the time I did finally nut, I'd have to be careful the force didn't knock her skull square off her shoulders.

Never seen it happen but there was always a first time for everything, am I right?

I swung my legs out as far as they would go and slid my ass lower on the seat. My head tipped towards the ceiling as she did that thing some broads did with their cheeks that turned their mouths into Hoover vacuums and had even the most church-going girl sucking cock like a two-dollar whore.

Didn't know if it was learned, like riding a bike, or just a natural God-given talent. Either way, this Catholic boy would have easily turned heathen given the choice. I mean, if Eve blew Adam before handing him that apple, I sure as shit couldn't blame him for eating it. Guy probably needed the nutrients.

The longer Charlee went, the fewer brain cells she left behind till the fogginess had nothing to do with the pan I took to the side of the head and everything to do with the throat taking my cock to the larynx.

I heard a gurgling sound, and I didn't know if it was me choking on blood or Charlee choking on my dick. I didn't care either 'cause I was five... four... three... two seconds away from coming. My balls rising as quickly as a church pew on Sunday when the game was on. Charlee taking me down—all the way down—gliding her mouth all the way back up again and...

Gone. I opened my eyes. She was gone. Not gone, gone. But not... *on*.

She used a thumb to wipe the saliva from the sides of her lips and pinned me with a smirk. "You said you weren't here to fuck me. I'm just making an honest man outta ya, Mr. Dawson."

CHAPTER SIX
CHARLEE

"I ... what?" Jack sputtered. "I wasn't... That wasn't..." He shook his head from side to side. "That's not the same."

"It's not?" I clutched a palm to my chest, those imaginary pearls nowhere to be found. "Well, butter my buns and call me a biscuit... Guess I always assumed someone named it oral *sex* for a reason."

"I, no, I wasn't the one who... You were the one who was..." He squirmed in his seat while I pried a stray pubic hair out of my teeth with the end of my pink polished nail. I flicked it off before tapping that same finger against my temple.

"Ohhh! I get it now. It's not about the motion of the ocean." I rotated my hips—slow, sensual-like—and raked my teeth against my lower lip before adding, "It's about whoever's steering the bow. And here I was, thinking it was more about penetration. You and your little…" I gestured a hand towards his lap. "…corn cob entering my… corn hole."

I grinned. There was only one thing more amusing than a guy who needed to pound his chest and scream about what big a man he was, all while acting like a *man-sized* toddler. And that was a guy who pretended like he had the higher moral ground.

Kick the box out from under him, though, and he'd land on his ass like the rest of us.

I glanced down at the matching red friction burns on my lower legs. Ass? Knees? However you landed, it was all the same. I mean, I knew I wasn't perfect. What I was, was reactionary. Take from me, I take from you. In some form or another. And right now, I was taking that orgasm this here pickle-diddler claimed *he didn't want.*

"The thing is…" I hummed. "An open door doesn't mean someone's inviting you in any more than an open mouth means I'm willing to blow you. To completion at least."

"I don't understand…" he muttered while trying to hide his discomfort.

The way his rooster was throbbing and bobbing between us was a clear sign he wasn't doing a good job of it. Thing looked so red and angry it might as well climb up onto the rooftop and start crowing.

"What does that have to do with anything? Your door was closed," he tried to rationalize.

"Actually it was locked." I shrugged, crossing the room to lower my boiling pot to a simmer. Then I tugged open the drawer to my right, fumbled around with the contents until I found what I was looking for, and waved the bundle of plastic zip ties in the air.

Jack glanced from my face to my hand, his body deflating in more ways than one. "Charlee, what are you gonna do with those?" he asked, even though we were both well aware he wasn't gonna like the answer.

I quirked an eyebrow, a smirk teasing at one side of my mouth as I yanked a single zip tie free and looped it together before rotating it around the tip of my finger a few times.

"Wrangling myself a rooster," I replied.

CHAPTER SEVEN
JACK

I stared down at the makeshift cock ring currently strangling the fuck out of the base of my dick and yanked at the bindings around my wrist for the millionth time. They didn't budge.

When I glanced back up, Charlee was watching me, her fingers plucking a thin strip of fabric from somewhere inside her booty shorts and dragging it along one leg, then the other, before she kicked it off her ankle with the end of a boot heel. Neon-pink, triangle-shaped fabric that covered about as much as me standing up and trying to wrap that dishtowel dangling over the edge of the sink around my waist instead.

The crotch part was soaked. I could smell it from across the room. The distinct odor of thigh sweat and pussy juice. Which told me she liked sucking me off almost as much as I liked her doing it.

I didn't hate the idea of being used like a human fuck doll. At least not at first. Chick was edging dangerously close to the "not worth the trouble" side of the crazy-hot scale, though. The kind of hot that had a guy wetting himself twice over and the kind of crazy that had him waking up the next day with no memory of how he ended up in that ice bath—*ya know, the dark web kind of crazy.*

I opened my mouth, a few choice words making their way up my throat when something soft and frilly was shoving 'em back down again. That same piece of fabric she called underwear as Charlee rested a hand behind me and lowered herself onto my lap. Her shorts shoved to one side and her pussy lips sucking me up inside her like the nozzle attachment of my ma's old horizontal vac.

Only tried that shit once as a teen but once was more than enough for me to make the comparison. This was a lot warmer if I were being honest. Wetter. But just as painful as she began bouncing up and down on top of me.

The harder I got, the faster she went, and the better and worse it felt. The little piece of plastic keeping my cock from being able to deflate, no matter how much pain I was in, and the smirk on her face telling me she wasn't stopping.

Charlee looped her arms around my neck, humming to herself as she shucked off her boots and used the tips of her manicured toes to guide her back-and-forth motion. Grinding instead of pounding until my cock turned the same shade as a lump of hamburger meat. The purple kind of red. Her juices seeping passed the opening in my fly and soaking my thighs when she rose up one last time and sank all the way down to my balls, while her cunt throttled me just as tightly as the piece of plastic that was still preventing me from coming.

"Fuck," I hissed out.

Charlee pulled all the way back, rolled onto the balls of her bare feet, and pushed off me. She reached out and flicked my cock with the tip of one of her talon-like nails before pivoting back around towards the hall.

"Hey! Where are ya going?" I called out after her.

"I'm fixin' to take a nap," she called back.

"And what about me?" I nudged the chair forward a few inches, only to have one of the legs snag on the table's edge.

"Why, Mr. Dawson, are you asking to come to bed with me?" She blinked at me over a shoulder. "What kinda girl do ya take me for?"

CHAPTER EIGHT
CHARLEE

A real nutter, that one.

She's certainly a bit touched in the head, ain't she?

Who? Oh, Charlee? Our Charlee? Yeah, girl's crazier than a road lizard. Just ask the Mitchells' boy. Shame what happened to 'em.

Not to speak ill of the dead but I heard her ma killed a fella.

I heard it was two... And ya know what they say... Like mother, like daughter.

Poor girl never had a chance, did she? Bless 'er heart.

I stretched my arms high over my head with a loud yawn, my stomach fussin' as I climbed off the bed and padded my way back into the kitchen. I'd left an entire pot of Philip to rot on the stove. I hated wasting good food. Then again, there *was* more of 'em where that came from.

Plenty of Tyler and Kevin and Bruce too.

I'd also forgotten to flick the switch off before going to bed, and the overhead light caught on the shiny stainless steel appliances as soon as I stepped around the counter. I glanced up at my reflection in the microwave window and shuddered at the girl staring back at me. Runny mascara, flat curls, bags under her eyes for days.

Yep, I looked about as limp as a dish rag. Which reminded me...

My fingers trailed over the large wooden knife block to my right until they found the scissors. I tugged the handle free and tiptoed over towards the kitchen table, careful not to wake my house guest. His chin touching his chest, slowly rising each time he took a shallow breath and let it out again. His long, black lashes fanned out against each of his cheeks—one slightly more swollen than the other from where he landed on his face after I'd struck 'em with the pan.

Didn't seem fair that men always had the sorta lashes us gals had to paint and pluck and preen for.

But life's not fair, Charlee, my ma's voice reminded me.

I rolled my eyes as I kneeled in front of the chair to get a better look while my hand crept closer to rest the sharp edge of the scissors against the base of the nice serving of man meat that shouldn't have had my mouth watering like it was. And started snipping away.

Jack woke with a start and a shriek. His eyes popping out of his skull as he looked from my hand, to the scissors, and back to his lap. "What the fuck are you doing!"

"Best not to move right now," I hummed as I closed the scissors another few millimeters. He took in a deep breath, the sort that told me an ear-piercing scream was coming next, as I clicked the blades closed and yanked my prize free. "Now that wasn't so bad, was it?" I grinned.

Jack's face turned powder white, his eyes rolled back in his head, and then he was out quicker than the time the neighbor's dog found ma's whiskey stash.

And they said women were dramatic...

CHAPTER NINE
JACK

I woke to the feel of something standing over me with the added pressure of something else—something *sharp*—jabbing into the side of my head. Above my left eye. Which shot open only to be pressed closed by the tip of a pointy finger.

I took a deep breath and tried to relax until I remembered that same finger had been squeezing a pair of scissors against my crotch not all that long ago.

My eyes shot open again, and Charlee stepped back with a huff as I glanced from my lap to the needle in her hand. Back down to my lap one more time and over to the sliver of plastic zip tie curled up on the table.

I forced out a relieved puff of air through my lips and followed it with a chuckle. I was the only one laughing, though. Charlee was about as amused as I was when she came at my dick with that pair of scissors.

"Keep squirming and you're gonna lose an eye,

sugar." She popped a piece of chewing gum into her mouth before reaching forward and yanking my head back by a fistful of hair.

I stared up at her with a stupid grin on my face. "Better that than my cock."

"It is a good cock." She nodded once while pressing her nail on my left eyelid, holding it down as she continued to fix me up with what looked to be a pair of tweezers, a sewing needle, and some household thread.

"Glad you agree, babe," I grunted through the pain. For someone so little, girl sure was rough.

When Charlee was done piecing me together like one of those dollar-store craft kits that had more parts than instructions, she tapped the back of my head. I dropped it forward again, my neck muscles stiff as I shifted myself upright in the chair. I then watched as she tossed the needle in the trash bin, stashed her first aid kit in the cabinet under the sink, and started washing her hands. She dried 'em on a dishtowel before opening the fridge and setting a packet of lunchmeat on the counter. She grabbed for the bread next.

I cleared my throat, and she set her carving knife down on the cutting board. "'Preciate the special attention and all, babe, but how 'bout we put Jack Junior away for a bit."

Charlee glanced from the two dishes she was plating up on the counter to where I was jutting my chin towards my open fly and floppy dick. It was still a little red around the base, but other than that, not much worse for the wear. My balls on the other hand...

"Why? Is he shy?" She quirked a single eyebrow, pivoting around to drop one of the dishes on the table in front of me.

Before I could reply, she was bending forward, tucking me back into my boxers, and zipping me up a little too close *and fast* for comfort.

"Thanks," I grunted as she plopped down across from me with her own plate. And then she was shoving half the white bread and mystery meat sandwich into her mouth with the same finesse she'd used when she'd swallowed down my cock. Landing me with a glare my ma landed me with whenever I was playing with my dinner instead of eating it.

I craned my neck towards the table, as far as it would go, and took a few tentative sniffs. Could have been poisoned but something told me Charlee wasn't the poisoning sort. No, she was the type to look ya in the eye when she stabbed ya, and I was the type who was distracted enough by her tits to watch her do it—*but hey, so were most guys.*

I twisted in the chair so that one shoulder was leaning forward at the same time I lowered my head and stuck out my tongue towards the top of the sandwich. I gave it one good lick before Charlee was sighing, scraping her seat across the floor, and tugging it closer to me. Then her dainty little palm was closing against my throat as she guided my head in her direction while using her free arm to hand-feed me.

The first bite tasted like ash in my mouth. By the second, I didn't even care that the shit was dryer than my prom date's cooch after I told her I'd fucked her mom the morning before the dance.

What can I say? I was a seventeen-year-old boy with the sex drive of, well, a seventeen-year-old boy. And Mrs. Miller looked damn good for a woman pressing forty.

"Bologna?" I asked as I forced down the last bite of whatever the fuck I was eating with a mouthful of my own saliva. I would have sucked a dick for a tall glass of milk.

Not literally. I tried to clear my throat and ended up gagging on a piece of crust. *Okay, maybe literally. But that was a secret I'd take to my grave. Along with whatever was happening here.*

"Not bologna." Charlee shrugged as she licked her fingers clean till not even a crumb was left behind. Once again reminding me of the shit she'd done to my cock. It was sore, but I had to admit I didn't hate the idea of going another round. "It does have a first name, though," she muttered to herself.

"What was that?"

"Nothing." She continued to hum the Oscar Mayer jingle as she rinsed the dishes off before setting them in the drying rack.

A few seconds later, she was slamming a glass of tap water in front of me and dropping a straw in the center.

"In case ya get thirsty in the middle of the night." She grinned. Tapped me once on the cheek and pivoted back towards her bedroom again.

"Charlee! Come on, babe. You can untie me!" I yelled

out, knowing it didn't matter much. She'd already made up her mind.

Guess this "easy" grab and dash was turning into a slumber party.

CHAPTER TEN
JACK

I waited an hour after I stopped hearing Charlee shuffling around the bedroom before bracing my spine against the back of the metal chair and using all my strength to pop my left thumb out of its socket. I hissed out a breath, sucked in a lungful of air, and repeated the same thing with my right.

It didn't take more than a few yanks of my arms after that to tug my upper body free from the zip ties that had me bound to the seat for the last few hours. I moved on to my legs next and then I was stepping towards the front door. Where my phone and wallet were waiting for me in one of those decorative bowls.

I popped my thumbs back into place and swiped up my stuff, the floorboards unnaturally loud as I paused to tug at the doorknob. It didn't budge. Neither did the bolt above it when I tried to shift it aside.

I squinted my eyes until I could make out the little

padlock that kept me in as much as it kept everyone else out.

"Motherfucker," I grumbled to myself.

Old apartments like these weren't usually locked up like Fort Knox. It was why I'd been scoping it out for the last week. Most of the building appeared empty besides this unit. I also didn't think the resident was home. But here we were. In crazy town.

I spun back around and started searching nearby drawers for a key. I could break the door down, sure. But I was looking for a quick, quiet escape that didn't have everyone on the block reaching for their landlines. I mean, I didn't have much of a leg to stand on if the cops came calling, now did I?

Okay, here's what happened, officer. Sure, I was planning on robbing the place, but she kidnapped me before I could do it. So who's the real victim?

One look at my six-foot-three ass compared to her five-foot-whatever would have every pig on the street laughing in my face before tossing me in a jail cell. And not for nothing, I was far too pretty for prison. It was why I was here in the first place. Needed a fresh start. To pay off a few less-than savory characters and start over. Somewhere a hell of a lot less orange-jumpsuity, if ya catch my drift.

Yeah, and how's that working for ya, buddy?

Not so good. Thanks for asking.

It wasn't crazy to talk to yourself. It was crazy to waste your time answering, though. Especially when you needed to be looking for a way out of this *Southern Fried Homicide* house.

The dumbbell Charlee called a sandwich sat like lead in my stomach as I snooped through all the cabinets in the kitchen before giving up and turning down the hall. I knew I needed to stay focused but that shit was hard to do with a full bladder. So I slipped inside the bathroom, *carefully* opened my fly, and quickly relieved myself.

I wasn't ashamed to admit it felt about as satisfying as a good nut at this point. When I was finished draining one very-full lizard, I tucked 'em back into my pants. And almost ruined everything when I reached for the handle to flush.

I stared down at the yellow-brown pool in the pink porcelain bowl for a moment. It wasn't very gentlemanly of me to leave my piss water behind, but it wasn't very gentlemanly of me to rob a broad either.

Somehow this seemed worse, though.

I shook the weird moral dilemma from my head and crept back out the bathroom door, pausing when I realized there was only one spot left to look for the key. The bedroom.

I rubbed at the back of my neck, as much out of habit as it was to loosen the kinks. I wasn't a creep. I didn't go sneaking into girls' rooms at night. I didn't go rooting through their underwear drawers. At least not when they were home. And only when I was looking for jewelry and shit to hock. Not because I was sniffing it like some perv.

I mean, there was that one time a few years back... But that was different. Annie and me were a thing, and it's not pervy when it's the chick you're fucking. It's romantic.

Decision made, or something close enough to one, I drew the sign of the cross over my body, mumbled out a low "sorry, ma," and grabbed the knob to Charlee's door. I twisted it, leaning my shoulder against the frame as I quietly swung the hinge open. Just enough to slip through and stand at the foot of the bed.

Charlee didn't move besides the slow rise and fall of her chest. One arm resting above her head, the other tucked against her side. It was hard to picture the woman who'd busted me up the side of the face with a frying pan when she looked like this. So small, angelic, on a king-size bed covered in blankets and frills. Her mouth slightly parting when she sighed in her sleep and her lashes fluttering just enough to tell me she was deep in it.

I chanced a small step forward and peered over her comforter to get a better look at her tits, shaking my head and stepping back again when I realized what I was doing.

"Not a creep, sure," I muttered to myself, and Charlee shot up on the bed and reached for something on her nightstand. "Fuck!" I cursed and lunged on top of her before she could get whatever she was grabbing for.

Best case? Some pepper spray. My luck? A handgun.

I locked both of her wrists above her head in one hand while flicking on the lamp with the other, my full body weight pinning her thighs together and keeping her from wiggling free. I glanced from Charlee's face to the object on the nightstand.

I was wrong. It wasn't pepper spray *or* a gun.

"Are you gonna hurt me?" she whispered, as I tried to make sense of what I was looking at. My glare narrowing in on the fuzzy handcuffs and the rocket ship of a vibrator sitting next to ʼem.

"No, I'm not gonna hurt you. Are those—?" I grunted at the same time her knee shot up to hit me square in the balls. My *very tender* balls.

CHAPTER ELEVEN
CHARLEE

"Buck all ya want, cowboy. I happen to be an expert bull rider." I brushed my lips against Jack's ear before leaning up and shooting him a wink as I shimmied lower. Then a little bit lower and lower still, enjoying the friction it caused beneath my nightgown and against my bare bottom.

I paused the back-and-forth motion to eye Jack from where *I* was now the one straddling *his* waist. Each of his arms secured to the metal rails of my headboard. Pinched so tight that the only thing a couple of dislocated thumbs would earn him was an eight-count and a hefty bar tab. And maybe a cold cot in the county lockup if this cowboy couldn't hold his liquor.

The fuzzy pink cuffs I kept on my bedside table weren't just for show. Though a gal could get used to the view.

I tilted my head to the side and watched the way

Titanic Boy's shirt lifted to reveal a decent rack of ribs—*I mean abs*—and a deep V that had my fingertips skimming his waistband on their own.

Jack yanked one more time on his left wrist. Hard enough to have me bracing myself on his pec with a palm. I flopped down in response, until I was flush against him, my elbows digging into his upper torso while I kicked my feet in the air between his legs as I stared up at him through my lashes.

He dropped his chin to glare back at me. "This isn't funny anymore, Charlee."

The rumble of his chest traveled up my arm and out my fingers. "From where I'm sittin', I think it's pretty darn hysterical."

Another tug and I was face-first between his man cleavage, cackling the more he cussed in my direction.

I shifted my left hand from where it was resting on his thigh now and trailed it across the front of his jeans until he was groaning and thrusting against my palm without meaning to do either. Then, when he was nice and distracted, his eyes closed and his head thrown back, I slipped two fingers into his front pocket.

"Is that a phone I'm feelin' or are you just happy to see me, Mr. Dawson?" I pulled the device free and tossed it across the room before positioning myself upright. "Oh, look at that! It's both!"

I grabbed for his belt, tugging it by the tail like a rattler in my mama's rose garden, and tossed that aside too. It hit something behind me with a *thwack* I didn't bother checking the origin of as I shucked the pillows off the bed.

His shoes were the next to go, one foot at a time, followed by his socks and then his blue jeans. Until the only thing standing between me and a full slab of raw, unmarinated man meat was an undershirt and a thin pair of plaid boxers that probably had his name written across the back in block lettering.

I catfished a hand into the little slit in the front and peered up at Jack through my lashes again. "Gotta safe word, sugar?"

He scrunched his nose at me but he didn't say to stop. I shrugged a shoulder and squeezed once.

"Charlee, stop it." *Oh, darn.* He waited until I was looking at him before adding, "How long do you plan on keeping me here?"

I huffed out a breath and crossed my arms over my chest. I quickly dropped them back onto the mattress as I crawled lower on the bed. My lips crotch level. My breath warm and raspy. "Wanna leave so soon, Mr. Dawson? And here I thought we were just getting to know each other."

He lifted his hips to meet me like he did in the kitchen, and I didn't wait for him to argue this time as I nudged my nose inside his boxers and licked him from tip to torso. He growled deep in his throat like a grizzly and I pulled his underwear down his ass. They landed somewhere on my bedroom floor while I landed myself back between his thighs, my mouth spread wide around the base of a nice piece of thick sausage.

My mama always did say that my eyes were bigger than my stomach, and I guess in this instance she was right.

I had a healthy appetite and I enjoyed all flavors... but I had to admit this particular one left a different sort of taste in my mouth. The sort that had my panties wet and my nipples peaked. The sort that had me moaning and the man beneath me groaning and meeting my face dip for dip. Stroke for stroke. Deep dive for deep dive.

I swiped out a hand, fumbling with the bedside table until my fingers brushed over the silicon top. One quick yank and the suction cup bottom popped off the veneer. Another flick of a thumb and my favorite battery-operated boyfriend was buzzing to life against my lady bits in a way that sent a shiver up my spine and out my mouth on a satisfied sigh.

I wasn't usually the one being spit-roasted alive, but now that I was, I understood what all the fuss was about. My screams more muffled than the ear-piercing shrieks I was used to hearing die out beneath the crackle of the fire. My body burning up in an entirely different way as I ground my hips against my pretty pink vibrator and Jack ground his against my heated cheeks.

I'd just started to taste the hint of something salty in the back of my throat, my legs quaking and my belly clenching when a few quick, hard thumps of metal against wood echoed past the bedroom door and into my ears.

Jack cussed, and I grinned around him as I plopped

his wet balls back into his lap like a hound dog playing
fetch, wrapped my silky robe around my waist, and went
in search of whoever was beating down my front door in
the middle of the night.

CHAPTER TWELVE
JACK

I looked at him, and he looked at me. One eyebrow cocked and a smirk teasing at the side of his mouth as he flicked the hot end of his flashlight back in my direction and then over to the fuzzy cuffs around each of my wrists.

"Care to explain what's going on here, son?" The bastard was trying to sound serious; instead, he sounded like he was two seconds away from popping a button on his uniform.

"Nothin' but a little harmless fun between me and the missus, officer." I clenched my teeth into a thin line, something resembling a grin. I think.

The pig standing behind him snorted into a cupped hand, his pen light flickering with the movement and blinding my left eye. I squinted back at them through the right.

"I see that." Officer Chuckles peered at his partner over a shoulder before turning to Charlee. "Care if we

have a look around just to make sure everything is in
order, Miss...?"

"Dawson," she replied, and I nearly choked on my
tongue. "Newlyweds." She grinned at the man, holding
up her left hand so that the diamond I sure as shit didn't
put there caught the light, while shooting me a sharp
glare that I *did* put there out of the corner of her eye.

Her grin was saying everything she wasn't saying.
You started it.

He nodded once and then he was shining that stupid
flashlight on my face again. "Why don't ya put some
clothes on and meet us in the living room, Mr. Dawson?"

"Love to, officer..." I wiggled my fingers at Charlee.
"Think you can lend me a hand, *dear*?"

Her smile dropped immediately. Mine widened.

"Of course, sugar," she hummed, pivoting on a bare
foot to trail a manicured nail down the buttons of the
pig's uniform. She flicked his name tag and then stared
up at him with what I was certain were doe eyes. "Go on
and help yourselves to the kitchen, Officer Bradley. We'll
be out there quicker than a cat on a tin roof."

Officer Bradley let out another low chuckle as he
waddled down the hall. Charlee watched him go for a
moment before clicking the door closed and switching
on the overhead light. Blinding me for the third time in
nearly as many minutes.

I blinked back the tears as she stomped towards the
bed, yanked the drawer open so hard it nearly came off
the grooves, and shuffled around until she found the
handcuff key.

She dangled it out in front of me as she glanced from the door to my face. I kept my expression neutral. "No funny business," she hissed.

"Ain't that a little pot meets kettle, babe?" I muttered as she climbed onto the bed, using my waist as leverage when she reached up to grab one of my arms. All while making a show of rubbing her cunt against my face.

Had to admit she smelled good enough to eat, though.

By the time my second arm was dropping onto the pile of pillows spread out on each side of me, I'd forgotten what it was I was supposed to be doing.

Oh, right, getting the fuck out of here.

I shook all those dirty thoughts from my head—at least I tried to—and brought my arms around the back of Charlee's waist. She lowered her face to meet mine and kissed me long and slow. Digging her teeth into my bottom lip when I attempted to pull away.

"Fuck me..." I grunted as I picked her up and set her down on her feet next to the bed. This broad was bad for my head whichever way you looked at it.

"Behave and I will," she fired back, curling her finger in my direction as she ushered me out the bedroom door.

A few more steps, Charlee in front and me trailing behind her, and we were standing in the middle of her little kitchen. She flitted around the stovetop, her silky robe twirling around her. Like none of this was weird.

I glanced down at myself and the pants I'd forgotten to put on. *All of this* was weird.

"Cream and sugar, officers?" She fluttered her

eyelashes at the two coppers standing in the living room, shining their flashlights in every dark crevice as if a crime scene was gonna just drop into their laps.

My eyes flicked over the splattering of dried blood darkening one of her kitchen tiles.

Then again…

"Two sugars and a splash of cream," Officer Bradley replied. "Please."

"Straight black for me, ma'am," his partner added.

Charlee set two mugs onto the kitchen table and shoved a third against my chest with another glare. She pulled out a seat for herself and then gestured for the pigs to join her. "So, what brings you to our door tonight, Officer Bradley?"

He crossed the room and slumped his ass in the first chair. "We got a call about an abandoned car out front. While we were running the plates, we caught ear of what we thought might be a disturbance." He cut me a sharp look. "Wanted to make sure everyone was all right."

"Right as rain, sir." I chuckled as I rubbed at the back of my neck. Cops always made me nervous. Cops at what was supposed to be my next burglary job made me suspicious.

"It was Mrs. Davis next door, wasn't it?" Charlee whispered.

"We really shouldn't say…"

"That's okay." Charlee winked as she reached out to run a finger over Officer Bradley's shirt sleeve. "She shouldn't have wasted your time. Y'all are so busy, fightin' the bad guys and keepin' us safe. I'll go over and talk to her tomorrow. Tell her not to bother you again."

"No bother, ma'am. Like you said, it's our job to protect and serve." The younger of the two tucked his flashlight back into his utility belt and dropped into the only open chair at the table. Tipping his hat before taking a long swig from his mug. "So how'd you all end up together?" He waved a hand between me and Charlee. "I'm a sucker for a good meet cute."

"Funny story actually." Charlee sighed, as though her crazy ass could really picture it. "It was kinda like he just showed up one day and never left."

"Charlee... that short for something?" Officer Bradley questioned.

"Nope." She popped her lips and slurped at her mug.

"Really?" I said without meaning to, and everyone's head snapped in my direction.

"Don't ya know your wife's name?"

I reached up a hand and rubbed at the back of my neck again. Didn't mean to do that either. "Heh, you know how it is once ya tie the knot, ya forget stuff."

"Anniversaries, sure. Not names..." Chuckles grunted.

"What kinda name is Charlee for a lady?" the younger guy asked. He took another chug of his coffee, paused, and stared at the inside of the cup.

"See! That's what I said!" I laughed, watching as the kid's head bobbed a little on his neck.

"Hey, Miss Dawson, did you put sugar—" His eyes rolled back in his skull and his forehead hit the kitchen table with a loud *thud* before he could finish speaking.

I looked over to Officer Bradley in time to watch his do the same.

I glanced down at my coffee mug—at the cream swirling around inside and the little granules sticking to my tongue—as my knees went weak and my stomach lurched up into my throat.

Guess I was wrong. Maybe Charlee was the poisoning type after all.

CHAPTER THIRTEEN
CHARLEE

"Get up, ya idjit." I cocked my head horizontal and kicked a polished toe out at Jack's side. He rolled himself onto his back with a grunt. "Keep fainting like that and I'm gonna think you're sweet on me or something."

"You poisoned me," he mumbled towards the ceiling, his arms spread out and his palms up. A grade-A martyr for the cause if I ever saw one.

Like I said, the guy was dramatic. But endearing in his own way too, I suppose.

"No, I poisoned them." I hitched a thumb over a shoulder. "You just got yourself a poor constitution, Mr. Dawson. Good thing you went and got yourself a fake wife while you were at it. She'll straighten ya out real quick. Now, come on and give a girl a hand."

I turned around and grabbed on to the smaller man's arm, tugging until his body hit the kitchen floor with a loud *thwack,* followed by a muffled *thump* when he flopped onto his face.

Jack scrambled to his feet to chase after me. "You killed a cop, Charlee," he hissed. "*Two* cops!"

I shook my head and spun back around to glare at him. "*No,*" I repeated. "I killed two guys dressed up to *look* like cops."

"What do you mean?" Jack was pacing the kitchen now. He was cute when he was frazzled.

Maybe I was the one who was sweet on him? That would be a first.

I quirked a brow. "Who do ya owe money to?"

"What?" His feet skidded to a stop. "I don't know what you're talkin' about. *You* don't know what you're talkin' about."

He was *less* cute when he was lying.

"Check their pockets." I crossed my arms over my chest, tapping an impatient foot while jutting my chin in the big guy's direction.

Jack huffed before stomping towards the table. "Yeah, and what am I checking for, Charlee?"

I lifted a single shoulder. "A wallet, a phone, something that ties them back to whoever it is that sent 'em to find you."

"No one is looking for me, babe. I ain't all that important." He fumbled around in the big guy's pocket and pulled a phone free. Tapping on the screen a few times before looking over at me again. "It's locked."

I rolled my eyes, took a fistful of "Officer Bradley's"

hair, and lifted his head off the table. Using my free hand to point at his reddened cheeks. Nature's rouge. Lividity was starting to set in.

"Oh, right..." Jack held the phone in front of the dead guy's face and waited for the screen to unlock. It didn't take more than a few seconds for his cheeks to take on a blush of their own.

"Told ya so," I sang out while collecting the cups and tucking them against my body with an arm.

"But I didn't say anything."

"You didn't have to." I twirled a finger in the air around Jack's head. *"That* said it all. So... who is it?"

"Who's who?"

I could feel him move up behind me as I deposited the cups into the sink. His breath against the back of my neck hot, his crotch region hotter. I grabbed a knife out of the chopping block to my right and spun around, using the tip of the blade to force him back a step.

"This thing between you and me is never gonna work if you aren't honest with me, sugar." I grinned, and Jack flared his nostrils. Gripping up my wrist with one hand and yanking me forward by my waist with the other.

"And what is this *thing* between you and me, babe? Sounds serious."

"Very serious," I hummed. "I don't kill for just anyone, ya know."

"You killed for me, though, huh?"

He squeezed until my fingers flexed and dropped the butcher knife, and I pushed up on my toes, leaning closer as I rubbed my stomach against his growing bulge. The one peeking out and tapping against my belly button.

"Is that your way of telling me you like me, Charlee—I just realized I don't even know your last name..." He lowered his head to meet mine, skimming his mouth over my lips. A kiss that really wasn't a kiss. But it wasn't *not* a kiss either. It was a challenge. A dare? And the thing with me was I didn't back down from dares.

"It's Dawson or did ya already forget, *dear*?"

Jack let go of my wrist, both hands shooting out to squeeze my backside as I jumped up and locked my legs around his waist. He shuffled a step, then another, nearly tripping over our friend on the floor as he spun us around to slam me against the door. And then his tongue was down my throat as he pounded up into me from below. My fingers switching from pulling on his hair to cupping his jaw. From cupping his jaw to clawing at his back. From clawing at his back to wrapping around and clinging to his neck.

I didn't want to just eat this man. I wanted to devour him. Taste him and savor him. Digest and absorb him.

"Ow, fuck," he grunted, and I opened my eyes to find myself teeth-deep in his shoulder. He didn't stop what he was doing, though. Just clenched his jaw and slapped a palm behind me, using the leverage to change up the angle.

I licked my bottom lip, the metallic tingle hitting my tongue as he continued to ram my lady bits against the door like a juicy piece of ribeye getting shoved into a meat grinder. And I relaxed my muscles and let him. I let him get me there all on his own.

One, two, three more flexes of those tenderloins and I was seeing tweety birds and ninja stars and Jack was carrying me back down the hall and dropping me on the mattress before diving back in again.

CHAPTER FOURTEEN
JACK

I was sleeping with a genuine serial killer. Literally. She curled up on top of me last night and fell asleep. Two dead cops in her kitchen and Charlee didn't have a care in the world.

Worst part? I didn't know if I was scared or turned on.

Probably both. I glanced down at the tenting in my boxers. *Yep, the answer was definitely both. Fuck, that shit was a lot to unpack.*

I pulled Charlee closer to my side and breathed in the scent of her strawberry shampoo. But I could do the *unpacking* later. Right now, I was content with being slightly less fucked-up than the woman I was holding in my arms. Arms that weren't cuffed to a headboard or zip-tied behind my back anymore.

"How did you know?" I asked, as the morning sun streamed in from her bedroom window, hitting me in the eye like the flashlight from a few hours ago. I squinted it closed and waited for my vision to adjust.

I felt like I'd been run over by a semi-truck but then, instead of putting me out of my misery, the driver of that same semi-truck had jumped down and fucked my brains out in the middle of the street.

So no harm, no foul.

"Know what?" Charlee grumbled against my chest. I knew she was awake the moment her breathing changed. She'd been pretending for the last twenty minutes or so, and I'd been letting her. Because she smelled nice.

"That those fuckers weren't real cops."

"My daddy was a cop," she replied on a yawn, pushing up on the mattress and stretching her arms above her head before peering back at me over a shoulder. "He taught me what to look for."

"Like what? What'd I miss?"

Charlee appeared to ignore me as she crossed the room, swiped her robe off the floor, and punched her arms through each of the sleeves. She was looping the tie around the middle when she finally looked over at me again. Head cocked and eyes so blue I swear I could have drank 'em up.

Might need to too. Woman damn near drained me dry.

"The patches for starters. There was no city or county listed, just the word police. Also, the badge number by his name wasn't real. It was six-digits. Should have been five—mhmm, maybe four—depending on when he was hired. Oh, and then there was the fact he was wearing Class A's. No real cop wears Class A's on patrol." She paused and tapped a finger on her chin. "Probably picked them up at a garage or estate sale or something, threw on a fake badge, and poof! He's got people like you willingly slapping on a pair of cuffs."

"Right." I dragged myself higher up on the bed to lean my back against the metal rails. "And what if you were wrong about all that?"

"I wasn't."

"But what if you were?" I tried again.

Charlee stopped what she was doing to stare at me. "Better for you to learn now, Mr. Dawson. I'm never wrong."

"Never?" I quirked an eyebrow, and Charlee walked over to my side of the bed, pinching my face between her fingers before giving my cheek a light slap.

"Never."

"Okay then." I grinned and pulled her down for a kiss.

A short one because she was already pressing a hand to my chest and prying herself free. "We have some bodies to dispose of. Come on now, they don't say the early bird buries the worm for no reason, now do they?"

"Who's they?" I shouted down the hallway, but she was already banging around in the kitchen. "Charlee, no one says that!"

I tugged my shirt higher up on my nose, trying to block out the smell of fresh blood. It didn't do much but it made me feel a little better.

"How d'ya know how to do that?" I pointed to where Charlee was bent over on the floor. Her mess of hair tied up out of her face and a pair of plastic glasses propped on the bridge of her nose. She wasn't wearing her robe anymore, having replaced it with a disposable rain jacket.

"My daddy was a butcher." She grinned at me from over a shoulder, red streaks splattering her face as she deconstructed our boys in blue as though they were Lego towers instead of full-grown bodies. Cutting the larger guy's limbs at the socket and popping them off just as easily as I popped off the wheels on my toy cars when I was little.

"Thought you said your dad was a cop?"

"Oh, Mr. Dawson, that's real unprogressive of ya to assume I only had one daddy."

"Riiiight," I muttered under my breath. Somehow a broad with her hands gut-deep in a guy's chest cavity was calling me the problem.

How the fuck did I get here?

"You broke in, remember?" she said even though I hadn't asked that shit aloud.

Charlee lifted the giant knife over her head and started hacking at the guy's throat with a lot less finesse than she used on his arms. A few more whacks and that was tumbling free and rolling across the room too. I stopped it with my foot and held my breath.

They didn't smell how I thought dead people smelled, but then again, they hadn't been dead all that long.

She jumped to her feet, grabbed Officer Bradley by the hair, and lifted him off the floor. "Now where do you think you're going, Mister." She laughed, and I snorted. "What's so funny?"

"Nothing," I told her.

She was cute. Even when she was just as fucking crazy. Which meant my ass was crazier.

"Sure seems like something, don't it, Chuck?" She looked from the head to me.

"Chuck?" I repeated.

"He looks like a Chuck, don't he?" Charlee shrugged, extending her arm so the head was dangling in front of us.

"Yeah, sure." I pushed the head back in her direction. "Officer Chuck Bradley. You got it, babe."

CHAPTER FIFTEEN
CHARLEE

"The knee bone's connected to the thigh bone," I hummed to myself while chucking *Chuck's* leg into the closest plastic tub. It rolled once and then settled in next to his torso. I tried to squash it down and it popped back up, a trickle of red leaking over the side. "The thigh bone's connected to the hip bone."

I took a step back, my palms braced on my hips, and eyed my handiwork. There were lot more pieces than I was used to keeping.

Lucky for us, I'd stocked up on those black hardware store bins with the neon-yellow lids and left 'em stacked in the shared basement *just in case* I was feeling particularly wronged by the male species on any given day. We'd hefted three of them up the stairs. But apparently, three wasn't enough for my friend here. Officer Bradley was thicker than a tick on a lake leech.

I brushed the cobwebs off my hands and stared at the

stack of body parts piled up over the lip before glancing towards Jack, who was watching me warily out of the corner of his eye. His arms crossed and his shirt stretched out around the collar from where he kept using it like a noseguard for no reason, seeing as the only thing rotten was his mood.

Kidnappin' and assault with a deadly weapon was peaches and cream. But kill a couple of fake cops and suddenly a guy starts lookin' at ya differently.

I sighed. Wasn't his fault, I suppose. This was new to him. It was just another day at my daddy's butcher's counter for me.

My gaze flicked to the side, and I grabbed Chuck's arm from the top of the pile and waved it in Jack's direction. "I sure could use that hand now."

He shook his head at me.

"I'm being serious." I flopped the arm disapprovingly, blood splattering across the tarps we'd laid out on the floor, before I tossed it back into the tub. "They ain't gonna keep like this."

When Jack continued to glare at me from where he was standing by the kitchen table, I took two steps forward and closed the distance, draping my arms over his shoulders. He lifted my safety goggles up onto my head. I smiled, and his cheek indented itself on one side.

"Yeah, and what do you suppose we do? Disposing of dead guys ain't exactly my area of expertise, sweetheart."

"I'm gonna have to phone a friend." I didn't like to do it if I didn't have to—independent woman and all—and it was much more lucrative to preserve the organs and keep ’em whole. But I knew a couple of quacks who were always looking to add a few spare parts to their human chop shop. Couldn’t tell ya what they did with ’em. Just that they didn’t ask questions. Which meant I didn’t ask ’em either.

Two birds, one stone. And that stone came with a stack of cash.

“Mmm, pretty certain the fewer people who know about that...” Jack stretched his neck and peered over my head at the tubs, shaking when a shiver went up his spine. “...the better.”

“Don’t go mansplaining murder to me, Mr. Dawson. One of us is a professional. The other one still has a frying-pan sized lump on the side of his head.” I tapped his temple with my index finger for good measure, and Jack winced.

“Speaking of...” He cleared the frog outta his throat, and I watched the way his Adam’s apple bobbed in front of me. “How many times have you done this, exactly?”

I blinked up at him, my lashes fluttering like mama taught me to do whenever I wanted a new toy from the corner store and daddy said we had to tighten our purse straps.

“Are you asking me my body count?” I gasped while pressing a hand to my chest.

“Ah, yeah, you could call it that?”

I grabbed Jack’s cheeks and gave them a quick squeeze between my fingers before pushing off him and walking towards the bathroom. "A lady doesn't kiss and tell! What I will *tell* ya is that I've never done two in the same sittin'." I winked at him over a shoulder and kept walking.

"Charlee, I didn't ask if you kissed them," he yelled out by the time I was reaching an arm inside the stall and turning the shower on. He appeared behind me a few seconds later. One hand on the doorjamb as he swung himself into the room. "Wait... did you kiss them? Are you into that kinda thing?"

"What kinda thing? Gettin' my rocks off with dead guys? No one likes a sour pickle, Jack." I had to pinch my lips to keep from laughing. I took a deep breath and schooled my features.

His eyebrows scrunched up in the middle like he was thinking too hard. "Aren't all pickles sour, Charlee?"

"It's just a saying." I rolled my eyes, a hand on my hip and my hot water swirling down the drain. "Seriously? What's next? Ya gonna ask me if I cook 'em up and eat 'em too?"

He paused to stare at me for a moment, his eyes bouncing from side to side like a ball across a ping-pong table. Then he shook his head. "'Course not."

"Good, 'cause I gotta get all this blood cleaned up unless you'd prefer to lick it off?" I quirked an eyebrow at him, and Jack backed me into the shower stall. Clothes and all.

"Haha, very funny," he grunted, and then he was lifting me up by the hips and pressing me against the tile. The hot stream pelting against his back and the water turning pink as it bounced off my raincoat and dripped off my legs.

I wasn't joking. He didn't need to know that, though. Sometimes it was better to not know where all the bodies were buried. Most times it was better not to leave any bodies around in the first place.

CHAPTER SIXTEEN
JACK

"I'm sorry but I'm gonna have to kill ya."

My neck snapped in Charlee's direction as she stood over the stove and swatted at a fly buzzing around her head. I took a deep breath and nearly jumped outta my skin when she stabbed the insect into her cutting board with a paring knife. It kicked its little insect legs around a few times, and Charlee watched it struggle until it stilled.

Then she looked up and smiled at me. It wasn't the creepy smile you would think it to be, though. It was soft, her eyes sparkling and her cheeks pink and puffy like someone had just pinched 'em.

I shot her a wink, and she continued stirring the pot on the stove, only to glance towards the entryway a few seconds later when her little camera panel beeped, letting her know someone was at the door. Musta been how she got the drop on me that first night.

Of course my dumb ass would break into a serial

killer's house with a state-of-the-line security system. *Why the fuck not?*

"Kaz!" Charlee squealed at the same time she swung the door open and jumped into some blonde, tatted-up fucker's arms. She wrapped her legs around his waist, and he cupped her ass a little too familiarly as he walked her back inside.

"Hey, sugar tits. Heard ya got some…" His glare flicked to me before adding, "…parts for us."

She jumped down and gestured towards the storage bins we'd piled up in the corner, a bare foot sticking out of the one on top and a couple of fingers gripping the edge. Charlee said rigor mortis had set in. I didn't care to find out what that looked like.

"That's not parts. That's the whole damn thing." He laughed, and Charlee cocked a hip like she did whenever she was about to get sassy. Which was more frequent than not.

"And what are whole things made out of?" She quirked a brow. "*Parts.*"

"Got me there." The guy grinned, his attention shooting back over my way as he ran a tongue along his perfectly white teeth and jutted his chin at me. "Who's that?"

Charlee grabbed onto my arm and rested her head on my shoulder. "My boyfriend."

"You don't need a boyfriend if you wanna good fuck, sweetheart," he replied, that fucking stupid-ass grin widening. "You always got my number."

Charlee rolled her eyes before whispering out of the

side of her mouth, "He's kiddin'. Our mamas were cousins."

"Second cousins—*distant* second cousins," he corrected her, his eyes on me when he adjusted himself in his pants. "You gonna grab one of these bins or just stand there and stare at my cock all day?"

I stepped forward, my fists clenched at my sides, and Charlee tugged me back. Tony woulda bashed this fucker's face in already. But my girl could take care of herself. And this fucker. And me. Besides, I didn't want to draw any more attention from the nosey neighbors she'd mentioned—especially with a stack of body parts just hanging out in the kitchen.

"Ut-uh." Charlee shook her head. "This one's not allowed to leave."

"And why's that?" the guy asked.

"Because I kidnapped him." Charlee looked up at me and smiled.

"Thought you said he was your boyfriend?" He glanced between us, like suddenly we were more interesting than the crime scene he was here to clean up.

"He is." She shrugged.

"Aw, come on, little coz. You're far too pretty to be kidnapping boyfriends." The fucker closed the distance, pulling Charlee against his chest and spinning her around to face me. "I know your ma taught ya better than that. If a guy wants to leave ya, let him leave. There are plenty of other guys wanting to get into those pretty pink panties of yours."

I shoved him back a step and tugged Charlee into my

arms. "Hey, pal, how 'bout you back the fuck off," I gritted out. "I wasn't her boyfriend when she kidnapped me."

He dropped his grin until his expression resembled something that should be on a villain in a horror flick. His mouth pulled straight and his glare unblinking. Then, as if a switch had been flipped, he threw his head back on a loud cackle, one hand clutching his stomach and the other pointing at me. "Now that makes fucking sense."

I turned to Charlee and dropped my mouth to her ear. "This guy fuckin' serious?"

"Never," she said. "*Always,*" she added on a huff.

An hour or so later, Charlee's "cousin" and a big mute guy he brought with him were wiping up the entryway with a mop and some industrial-grade cleaner. When they were done, he reached into his pocket and tossed Charlee a tin can.

"For Mrs. Davis." He chuckled before strolling out the door with a weird skip in his step. My ma would tell me that guy was up to no good. I'd tell her, at this point, so was I.

I looked over at Charlee and the tin in her hand. "He brought your neighbor a can of tuna?"

Charlee nodded as she stepped up to the front door, swung it open, and called out, "Mrs. Davis!"

By the time she stepped back again, a white fluffball with a few patches of fur missin' was sauntering in behind her. Its tail raised and curled at the end as it rubbed against Charlee's legs.

"Mrs. Davis is a cat?" I asked, just to make sure I was understanding this right.

Another nod and a wider grin. "Also why I knew those guys were lyin'. Everyone on this block knows Mrs. Davis," Charlee explained.

I glanced down at the stray that was currently licking at a spot of blood Charlee's friends had missed on the floor. "Ain't that kind of a weird name for a cat? Does that mean there was a Mr. Davis?"

I laughed, and Charlee just stared at me as she plucked the cat off the floor and tickled its belly. "There was. But she ate him."

CHAPTER SEVENTEEN
CHARLEE

I held out a hand towards my cousin and tapped my foot while doing a grabby motion with my fingers. Like I used to do when we were kids and he skipped off to the corner store with the money he'd stolen outta my piggy bank. He'd always bring me back something too. But that wasn't the point. The point was he should have asked me in the first place.

Kaz wasn't one to ask for permission, though. He was more the type to press his luck and hope ya didn't notice.

He'd just returned from doing whatever it was he did with the bodies over at the crazy house he worked at. I didn't much care for the details and neither did he.

"Where's the rest of it, Kazmir," I said. It wasn't a question. Not really, seeing as we both knew he'd shorted me.

It wasn't about the money. It was the principle of the thing. No one got a pass. Not even family.

"Don't ya think I deserve something for my time, *Sharlotta*?" he countered, in that thick Russian accent he liked to use whenever he was tryin' to get under my skin by sounding like my daddy.

"It's just Charlee now, thanks." I rolled my eyes. "Now go on and hand it over before I serve ya up like your mama's *moskovskaya*." I used the same accent on him, and he tucked his hands into his pockets.

"Now we both know you wouldn't do that, little coz."

"Oh yeah?" I tilted my head to look him over from cheek to round-tip. "And why's that?"

Kaz shrugged a shoulder. " 'Cause we're blood."

"Ya know what? You're right. I wouldn't. But blood has nothing to do with it." I grinned while pointing a manicured finger at the ink that covered his throat and climbed up behind his ears. "It's 'cause tattoos taste like the underside of a donkey's rear."

My cousin barked out one of his obnoxious laughs and stuffed the rest of the cash into my open palm, and then he was turning around and walking towards the door again. I stopped him with a quick tug on his shirt, glancing over a shoulder to make sure that Jack was still holed up in the shower. I could hear the water running.

"Wait. I got a question for ya."

Kaz quirked an eyebrow, his gaze flickering over my head and likely doing the same thing. Making sure we were outta earshot of any busybodies. But there wasn't nobody 'round except Mrs. Davis, who was sleeping off her lunch next to my radiator—*and she wasn't telling on me unless I told on her. Girl code and all.*

"Go on and ask it. We ain't got all day, sugar tits." He flicked one of my nipples through my shirt, and I grabbed his hand and twisted until I heard it crack. Kaz didn't so much as flinch. My cousin didn't feel pain like a normal person. Which made breaking his bones slightly less gratifying than it normally would.

"Whatcha know about the Mulligans?" I pressed him.

"Buncha Micks, into the usual mob shit—pills, gambling, great if you wanna get your hands on the white stuff. Why? Finally looking to loosen up a bit?" Kaz nudged me with a shoulder before he gripped his dislocated wrist with his free hand and twisted it back into its socket like a cap on a pop bottle. "You don't need them if you're lookin' to party, Charlee. You know I gotchu."

"Not me," I grumbled as I pushed my cousin out the door.

He grabbed on to the jamb with both hands, his much larger frame keeping me from moving him more than an inch. "Ut-uh, I ain't leaving till the show's over. I wanna watch this."

I cussed under my breath, stomped towards the bathroom, grabbed Jack outta the shower stall by the ear, and led him into the kitchen bare-assed and dripping wet all over my floor.

I shoved him down on a seat cushion and shot him a glare. "Jack Alexander Dawson, what were ya thinkin' getting yourself mixed up with the Irish mob?"

He rubbed a hand over his ear and dragged the chair back to get a better look at me, his limp rooster sticking to a thigh as he spread his legs. "Who's starin' now?" He smirked at Kaz before turning to me. "And how do you know my middle name?"

"Your mama told me." I tapped my shoe like I'd tapped it at my cousin a few minutes earlier. "You still didn't answer my question."

"It ain't that serious, Charlee," Jack muttered, and I cracked him across the side of the head with an open palm. At least it wasn't a pan.

"*Ain't that serious*," I parroted, throwing my arms in the air. "It's serious enough for them to track you down all the way out here. How much?"

Jack lifted a shoulder, that dimple deepening in his cheek as he pulled me down onto his lap. Chest to back. "Not much."

I spun around to face him, straddling his thighs and locking my arms around his neck. "How much, Jack."

"Twenty grand," he replied, and my cousin let out a low whistle from behind us. "We don't need no comments from the peanut gallery," Jack hissed at him.

"Wouldn't dream of it." Kaz snorted. I peered towards the entryway and shot him a look that said what I didn't have to. He spun on the heel of his boot and grabbed on to the door. "Oh, but a little word of advice? Might want to ask your new girlfriend what she's got cookin' up in that pot over there."

Then my cousin slammed the door shut behind him, and I could hear 'em cackling all the way down the hall.

There were more than a couple of screws loose with

that one. Pretty sure his mama dropped him on the head when he was a baby. A few times.

"What's in the pot, Charlee?" Jack asked, and I turned my head back around to look at him.

"Hm?"

"I said... *what's in the pot, Charlee?*" he repeated.

CHAPTER EIGHTEEN
JACK

"What's in the pot, Charlee?"

"Hm?" She turned her wide eyes on me.

"I said… *what's in the pot, Charlee?*"

She started grinding her ass against my lap, my cock quickly rising to the occasion. I had to grab her hips to stop her.

"Charlee, what's in the fucking pot?" I asked her a third time.

She shrugged a shoulder. "Meat stew. It's my mama's recipe."

It wasn't what she said but the way she said it—like it was a question or there was some double meaning behind it—that had me sliding her off my lap and heading towards the stove. I lifted the lid and stared down at the mixture of meat, potatoes, and carrots. What appeared to be pepper flakes and some green stuff sprinkled on top. It didn't look different from any other stew I'd ever seen. It didn't smell all that different either.

But what the fuck did I know about stew? I grew up eating pasta seven nights a week while my pops knew better than to complain about it.

I could sense Charlee tiptoeing behind me, and could only hope she didn't have another pan in her hands as I tugged the fridge door open and scanned the contents. It was filled to the brim with packets of meat: sausages, flanks, ground, and chunk.

I swiped up the first thing my fingers brushed and read the label on top. *Tyler.* The next one. *Bruce.* And the next. *Kevin.* Then I turned around to look at her.

"Charlee, why do all these packages have names on them? Do you name your lunchmeat?" It sounded weird. But it was completely reasonable when you remembered this broad had a street cat named *Mrs. Davis.*

Charlee stared back at me with a blank expression on her face. I was joking, but suddenly shit didn't seem so funny anymore.

I assumed her cousin was fucking with me. Or, at the very worst, I'd find out that my girl had a taste for exotic animals like caribou or zebra or some other weird shit. Now I wasn't so sure.

When she didn't answer me, I glanced over into the pot again and watched as something floated its way to the top. It looked like a misshapen carrot or maybe a...

I jumped back from the stove, nearly knocking Charlee flat on her ass. "Is that a...?"

I closed my eyes, shook my head, and blinked 'em

open again. Then I chanced another peek into the pot. None of that changed what I thought I was seeing, so I grabbed a ladle out of the little cup thing on the counter and fished around the stew until I found what I was looking for. Dropping it back in as soon as I found it. And jumped back again.

"Yup, that's a fucking finger! Charlee, what the fuck?"

I snatched up each of her hands, counting off one digit at a time and then did the same to myself. All twenty of 'em were there. Twenty-one if you included the thumb still floating around in the pot.

"Charlee, babe, why do you have somebody's finger cooking up on your stove?"

She shrugged another shoulder. "I told ya I didn't sleep with 'em."

"I... um... You're right. You did." I combed a hand through my hair, quickly pulling my arm back to count my fingers one more time. Still all there.

Wait... one, two, three, four, five... Yup, all good.

I took a deep breath, my eyes bouncing from Charlee to the pot, from the pot back to Charlee, whose expression remained unreadable.

"You can leave now if you want." She spun around and walked towards her front door, opening it wide and gesturing for me to step through.

Mrs. Davis glanced up from where she was curled up in a ball of white fur, stretched out her legs, and pranced out the door with a swipe of her patchy tail.

I stomped over but instead of walking out with the

cannibal cat, I slammed the door shut and slid the lock back in place.

Was I stupid for not following her?

Probably, but I was stupid and curious. It was something that always got me in trouble growing up.

I grabbed Charlee by the wrist and guided her over to the kitchen table, forcing her to sit down like she had done to me when she'd dragged my naked ass out of the shower. Which reminded me I was still walking around the house in nothing but a towel.

That would have been a hard one to explain if I had decided to walk out of here. Not as hard as explaining a girlfriend who liked to eat people. Literally. But still fucking awkward. Besides, I didn't even know where she'd stashed my car keys.

Maybe her telling me to leave was more of a gesture than anything else? Or a test. Either way, I wasn't too worried about passing it.

I lowered myself onto the chair across from her and took another deep breath. Okay, several deep breaths. This was a lot to take in.

Your girlfriend being a serial killer was one thing, but a serial-killing man-eater was a-whole-nother.

Don't ask me why. It just was. *It was!*

"All right, how 'bout you explain it to me." I nodded once, and Charlee peered up from her hands to look at me. "Do you... uh... like the way it tastes?"

"What?"

"Humans. People, Charlee. Is it a taste thing? Like preferring steak over chicken?"

She tilted her head and appeared to consider my words. "No."

"Okay… then what is it? I am really trying to understand here, babe. Can you explain to me why you do it? Please."

"Why?" It wasn't a dumb question. I was questioning it myself. But that didn't mean I had an answer for her either. Other than…

"Because I'm starting to like you, Charlee Dawson."

She smiled up at me, those eyes of hers just as bright and blue as I remember them being the first time I saw them. In this kitchen. In this chair.

CHAPTER NINETEEN
CHARLEE

Why?

No one had ever asked me that before. Not my papa. Not my cousin. Not even that one guy I'd made sit and watch me cook up his pinkie toe before I removed the bone and popped the fleshy bits between my teeth like a piece of chewing gum. But that coulda been because he'd passed out from the shock first.

Honestly, I didn't think about it all that much. The reason I did what I did or if I even liked doing it. It was second nature. One girl rightin' all the wrongs everyone else was too scared to right themselves.

It was also my moral obligation. Ya see, Mama had taught me that the higher the hair, the closer to God we'd be. And sometimes God was vengeful. He needed to be, else how was he gonna keep his flock from wandering astray?

I supposed *that* was the part I enjoyed the most.

Teaching 'em all lessons their mamas certainly didn't teach 'em like my mama did with me.

We hadn't had a lot growing up. Me and Kaz. My mama spent so much time scrimping and saving, just to make sure we were fed, and his mama was always working. So were our daddies. That was why nothing ever went to waste in our house and it wouldn't go to waste in mine neither.

It was as simple as that. Or maybe it wasn't simple at all if ya didn't know what it was to go to bed with your tummy rumbling. Sorta made sense now why my cousin was so extra. Extra food in his belly, extra cash in his pockets, extra drugs in his veins. Kaz was making up for everything he didn't have before or was afraid he wasn't gonna have again. At least that was my thoughts on it. Not everyone was as easy to figure out.

I glanced over to Jack, who was looking at me expectantly.

If he had enough cash to give it to the mob, something told me he wouldn't understand where I was coming from. So I pushed up from my chair, grabbed hold of his hand, and dragged him off towards the bedroom.

Sex was universal. It didn't need understanding, which was why it was one of my favorite things to do... when I wasn't doing *other things*.

I took two steps into the room, tugged my shirt off over my head, and then yanked Jack's towel free—darn thing was hanging on for dear life anyway.

He didn't say nothing. Just watched me as I moved

around him and shoved him backwards onto the bed with a hand pressed to his chest. And then I was climbing him faster than sin on a preacher.

Jack groaned, grabbing my hips as I ground myself against his waist. "Charlee, we need to talk."

"I'm pretty sure we talked plenty in the kitchen," I told him, at the same time I gripped his rooster by the throat and sank down on it until it was weeping instead of crowing.

"You know what I mean," Jack grunted, but he was already thrusting up inside me, his eyes closed and his brows pinched together in the middle.

"I do know." I laughed as I got us both closer and closer to seeing those pearly gates while also ensuring we wouldn't be allowed past 'em. "And all I heard was how much ya like me, Mr. Dawson."

He thrusted upwards one more time before flipping me over onto my back, never losing traction as he stretched my arms high over my head and held them there with one of his fists.

"I do like you, Charlee. Probably more than I should. Probably more than's good for me," he grunted into my ear.

"Okay..." I gasped when he started pounding me so hard one of my girls bounced up and nearly took me out. "I still don't see the problem."

Jack slid his knee off the mattress and stood to his full height, with two feet firmly planted on the floor and one palm on each of my thighs, as he slowly pulled back and drove in again. All his focus now on the way my lady bits swallowed him up and spit him back out. Swallowed him up and spit him out.

I could do the same thing and he'd be none the wiser. 'Cept, for once, I didn't want to.

He threw his head back and started driving forward faster, his breaths coming out in quick pants. "The problem is…" he huffed. "…you eat people, Charlee, and I'm not sure how I feel about that."

I was close but I could tell Jack was closer. So I sat up on the bed and pressed down on his shoulders, until his rooster popped its head free and Jack was kneeling in front of me.

"Then how 'bout you eat me and we call it an even trade?" I grinned wider, and Jack frowned. "What? Too soon?"

"Yeah, can we lay off the euphemisms till there isn't a finger slow-cooking on the stove anymore?" he grumbled before doing the same thing he was so concerned about me doing to everyone else.

He ate me alive.

Three orgasms later, two for me and one for Jack, I was rolling off the bed and waddling towards the kitchen. It didn't take more than a few minutes for Jack to come padding in after me.

I peered over at him from where I was cutting up a loaf of bread on the counter. "Hungry?"

"Starving." He propped himself up against the wall, crossed his arms, and watched me.

I nodded, grabbed another dish from the cabinet, and set it out beside the cutting board. The stew had at least two hours to go before the flesh was falling off the bones. So I plated up two sandwiches and handed one to Jack.

He took it out of my grip, raised the bread towards his mouth, and paused to look at me. "Hey, Charlee, what was in that sandwich you made me?"

I bit down into my own bread, mustard squirting out and spraying one side of my face. I wiped it away with a piece of paper towel and found Jack still staring at me. His food untouched.

"Charlee… it wasn't bologna, was it?"

I lifted a shoulder. "I already told you it wasn't."

CHAPTER TWENTY
JACK

I hated to admit it, but there were several advantages to being a newly-turned vegetarian dating a cannibal. *Before ya judge me, hear me out!*

First off, our grocery bill was much lower than most people's. And in this economy, we'd take all the help we could get on that one. Secondly, she never stole my leftovers and I certainly never stole hers. It was refreshing to open the fridge and see my Tupperware dish exactly where I'd put it the day before. And thirdly, blood made for great fertilizer, which meant my little homegrown garden was thriving.

Did it freak me out every time I thought about where that blood came from? Sure. So I decided to just not think about it.

I glanced out the kitchen window at where my tomatoes were popping up next to Charlee's rose bushes. They were companion plants the broad at the nursery had explained. Aesthetically different but each served their purpose. Kinda like me and my girl.

Charlee was the twisted chaos, a little prickly on the outside but so pretty to look at. She smelled nice too. And I was a giant lump of tomatoes. Perfect to grind up and throw in a pot of gravy if she got tired of dealing with my BS. Or at least that's what she liked to tell me. I *liked* to think she enjoyed my company too much to do that.

I chuckled at the thought just as Charlee was pushing in through the front door with her usual dramatic flair. One hand on her hip when she slapped a stack of cash on the kitchen table.

"Done! Twenty big ones." She grinned, wrapped her arms around my neck, and tugged my face down for a kiss.

It'd taken us a little over six months to scrape together enough cash to pay back my gambling debts, but we'd done it. And I hadn't had the itch to play the ponies ever since.

Threats on life or limb from a girl I knew could deliver on them would do that to you. Just another reason this woman was good for me. She kept my ass on the straight and narrow, and I kept her from piling up too many of those tubs she had stocked up in the basement.

I placed a palm on each side of her waist and lifted her ass up next to the cash on the table. Charlee giggled, and I muffled the sound with another kiss.

I didn't know why she and I worked so well. Just that we did. Sometimes opposites really did attract. Same as my ma and my old man. No one in our families thought they belonged together either. She was Italian American and he was off-the-boat Irish. The two of 'em might as well have been oil and water when it came to agreeing on just about anything.

But not everything needed to make sense, I suppose. Dating the girl who beat ya upside the head with a frying pan and tied your ass to a chair certainly didn't. Then again, neither did dating the guy who broke into your house to rob you.

Guess we shared something in common after all. Piss-poor dating habits.

"I'll drop it off tonight," I told her while gesturing a thumb to the cash. I had an appointment to meet up with one of the Mulligan henchmen for the handoff.

It could have been a setup for all we knew. Though I was pretty certain that it wasn't. They wanted their cash just as much as they wanted a returning customer. They would only be getting one of those things from me. They just didn't know that any more than they knew what happened to the two guys they sent looking for me.

Charlee had mailed them an envelope with a couple of fingers and a note telling the fuckers to back off or they'd be next. She didn't think I knew about it, and I had no intention of bursting her bubble.

I liked how keen on protecting me she was. I also liked how riled up she got. It was as adorable as it was scary.

"I'll come with you," she insisted, and I gave her that

look. The one that said everything without saying nothing. "You know, in case I get hungry." She winked at me.

I shook my head. There was no talking her outta something when she had her heart set on it. So it was usually just easier to keep my mouth shut and agree.

"Speaking of?" she hummed. "When we gonna have your mama over for dinner?"

"Depends..." I quirked a brow at her.

"On what?" Charlee asked.

"On who's cooking..."

BONUS CHAPTER
SHARLOTTA

TWENTY YEARS PRIOR

My eyes were glued to the lady on the television screen. The way her bright-red lipstick curled across her face when she smiled down at me from the glass. Her eyes circled in blue and her hair white blonde and piled twice as high as everyone I'd ever seen in real life. I had no idea how she got her hair that high. Mine was flat and fell down my back in long waves.

Maybe she was magic. It sure seemed like magic to me. 'Cause whenever she moved, her sparkly costume would move with her, catching the light on the stage so that I was just as mesmerized by it as I was with her voice.

She had such a pretty voice. It was almost as pretty as she was.

My papa said women who dressed like that were stupid. But this lady didn't seem stupid to me. How could you be stupid when everyone was looking at you the way I was looking at her?

If anything, the ones looking were stupid. She was smart enough to be noticed. No one seemed to notice me unless I was doing something bad.

I tugged at the light-blonde curl on my shoulder, twirling it around and around until it started to come loose. I quickly dropped my hand and stared down at the lock of hair in my hand. Now that I thought about it, the color wasn't all that different from the lady's.

I wonder if my hair could be piled high on my head like hers one day?

My papa made a loud sound from his throat, and I glanced over to where he was sleeping on the sofa with an empty bottle in his hands. Last time he did that, he woke up angry and the cops came and took him away for a while.

He was back now, though. I sighed as I watched his chest puff out and flatten down.

Sometimes I pretended my papa was one of those cops arresting bad guys—like the one who was here that last time and showed me all the parts of his uniform while my mama talked to his friend. Or maybe my papa could be like the nice man at the meat market, who always smiled when my mama and I came to visit. He'd sneak me a piece of cheese whenever mama wasn't looking. Or maybe I could just get a new papa. I'd be okay with anyone who wasn't like my real papa.

Sometimes I pretended I wasn't me too. The other kids didn't like me. They said my name was weird and that I talked funny. I was working on talking less funny so they would like me more—even though my mama said I shouldn't do anything just to make someone like me.

My mama was usually right but I wasn't so sure about that one. If the other kids didn't like me, they wouldn't invite me to come play with them.

Papa grunted in his sleep again, and I turned back to the lady on the screen. Dolly Parton. Her name flashed across the bottom of the television in big letters when she was done singing about some other lady who took her man.

If that were me, I'd say she could keep him. Men seemed like a lot more trouble than they were worth. My mama was always tired or sad or angry because of a man. Because of my papa.

Like right now. I could hear her clanking around in the kitchen, making dinner for us. I liked my mama's cooking, especially when we were lucky enough to have some leftover meat stored in the freezer. Didn't matter what kind it was, my mama knew how to make it taste good anyway.

Miss Parton was singing another song. Singing was my favorite way to practice my English so I crept over to my papa's chair and went looking for the remote to turn the television a little louder. Not loud enough to wake papa but loud enough so I could try to hear all the words and say them right.

I liked how Miss Parton said her words. Her accent was much softer than mine was, friendly too, like she was the sort of lady to bake apple pies at Christmas time. My stomach grumbled at the thought.

I took another step closer to my papa, and the floorboard creaked. I didn't think it was that noisy but my papa must have thought differently, because he jumped up and grabbed my arm, squeezing and twisting. I didn't cry though. My papa said crying was weak, and I wanted to be strong like my mama.

I bit down on my cheeks and let out a low whimper before I could stop myself. My mama came running into the room with a giant knife in her hand. My papa started yelling and cursing at her. My mama didn't say a word. She just looked him in the eye. My mama was small but she had a temper. She just never used that temper on me.

My papa lunged forward. He was too slow because of that empty bottle. My mama didn't drink any of that bottle so she was much quicker when she raised the knife high over her head and brought it down into my papa's chest.

He looked at it and then back up at my mama before he tipped over and dropped onto the floor. Landing on that same creaky board with the nail sticking out of it.

My mama nodded once and then turned her head towards me. *"Ty v poryadke?"*

"I'm okay, Mama." I smiled up at her and nodded back. "I'm gonna be just like Miss Dolly Parton when I grow up."

"You can be whatever you want to be, Sharlotka," she said. "But first you have to eat your dinner." Mama glanced at where my papa was twitching on the floor. "We're having meat stew."

ACKNOWLEDGMENTS

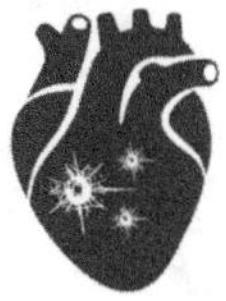

Thanks to everyone who has been a part of this long-ass process. To everyone who has shared, liked, commented, and preordered. To those of you who took a chance on me and my fucked-up brain. And to those who love the fictional characters that live rent free in my head. I could not have done it without you, and I am so very humbled.

I also wanted to say thank you to my ARC readers, who are taking time out of their busy schedules to read and review my book. And thank you to those of you who went as far as to read and review my prior publications too—I see you and I am so grateful for you.

ALSO BY SYBIL KNIGHT

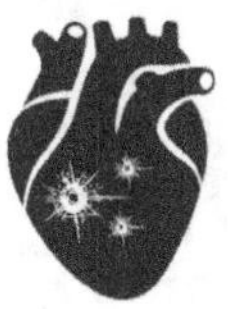

THE TRUTH AND LIES DUET:

T‍HE H‍ARSHER THE T‍RUTH

T‍HE S‍WEETER THE L‍IES

THE RENEGADES SERIES:

S‍KIN

L‍AMB

B‍ELLS

STANDALONE NOVELS:

H‍ALF C‍OCKED

K‍ILL J‍OY

STANDALONE NOVELLAS:

The Sins of Our Fathers

V Card

I'll BE Seeing You

The More the Merrier

Eat Your Heart Out

Nutcracker

More titles to come...

ABOUT THE AUTHOR

SYBIL IS A TRUE EAST COASTER WITH A LOVE FOR TRUE CRIME AND CAFFEINE. WHEN SHE ISN'T WORKING OR WRITING, SHE IS TALKING ABOUT WORKING OR WRITING.

HER STORIES RANGE FROM GRAY TO BLACK, WITH DARKER THEMES THROUGHOUT. SHE PREFERS HEROINES WITH A KICK-ASS MENTALITY AND THE HEROES WHO KNOW HOW TO REIN THEM IN. THE MENTAL AND MEDICAL ASPECTS OF HER BOOKS ARE WELL-RESEARCHED, THOUGH THEY ARE GIVEN A HUMANISTIC APPROACH AND DIAGNOSES AREN'T THE FOCAL POINTS. SHE BELIEVES HER CHARACTERS DON'T NEED TO WEAR LABELS IN ORDER TO GET THEIR MESSAGES ACROSS.

HER BOOKS ARE MOSTLY STANDALONES, THOUGH HER CHARACTERS MAY INTERACT AND INTERSECT WORLDS. ADDITION-ALLY, SHE WORKS CLOSELY WITH AND WRITES ALONGSIDE AUTHOR DAHLIA REIGN AND SOME CHARACTERS WILL APPEAR IN CAMEOS IN EACH OF THEIR PUBLICATIONS.

Sybil welcomes emails from readers if there are concerns or questions regarding any of her publications.

Email: authorsybilknight@gmail.com